Max to the Rescue

All Rights Reserved
Text and Illustration copyright 2022
by Lindsey Dutfield

Max the pony was very small.

He didn't seem to grow at all.

The other ponies were much
bigger,

Even his best friend Trigger.

When they went to the field to graze

At the lush clover, the big ponies would gaze

But Max could fit between the fence

And fetch clover for his friends, it made good sense.

In the corner of the field was a big tree
Where sweet juicy apples grow for free
But little Max was too small to reach
So Trigger picked them, one for each.

In Farmer John's garden the carrots were grown.

"They look so sweet and perfect", the big ponies moan.

So Max found a hole in the hedge and squeezed through

And brought back some carrots, for his friends to eat too.

Now his friends were all happy, but Farmer John was not

He had been watching as Max carried out his plot

"So that's where the carrots are going" he thought

And went to the shop and pony carrots he bought.

When night-time arrived the ponies came back inside

Fresh carrots were found in their troughs and beside

Them a big juicy apple for each pony's tea

How clever you are Max, to make Farmer John see.

Now Max was tiny and didn't eat much food

So he gave half his tea to the rabbits, so as not to be rude.

The rabbits were so happy, they jumped up and down

"When you need a favour just ask", said Pa Bunny Brown.

Now the next day was sunny and the ponies wanted to play
"Lets play racing", said Trigger, "I could gallop all day"
Tiny Max couldn't play this, as he couldn't keep up
"I'll be umpire". he said, "and present the winners cup".

So off raced the ponies, out the farm, up the hill, to the wood

With Max watching closely or the best that he could

Then back to the farm, thundered ponies flat out

All wanting to win, of that there was no doubt.

Now Prince, Belle and Trigger came in one, two, three.

But someone was missing and hadn't returned to the apple tree.

Max looked around frantic, "Where's Polly", he screamed

Then he raced up the hill. "I can gallop", he beamed.

When he got to the wood it was dark with no sunlight

And Max couldn't see Polly's coat of pure white.

"Polly", he shouted, "Where are you? Have you fell?"

When at last he heard a whinny and saw her in a dell.

Polly lay in a valley all covered in brambles.

Her beautiful mane looked a real shambles.

"Are you hurt or just stuck", asked Max, all concerned.

"I'm stuck and the brambles hurt", tiny Max learned.

Being tiny, Max managed to crawl underneath

The big bramble bush and chew the tough plant with his teeth.

But his teeth were not sharp and he couldn't bite through.

So he scrambled back out and tried to think what to do.

Rabbits have sharp teeth

Then all of a sudden it became very clear,

What he needed was rabbits and he needed them here.

So he raced to the farm and neighed for all to go to the wood

And Max went to the rabbits to ask help, if they would.

The rabbits were delighted to help their new friends
And they jumped up on Max and clung on through the bends,
As the brave tiny pony raced back to the wood
To free poor Polly pony as quick as they could.

The rabbits gnawed straight through the brambles with ease

And soon Polly was able to get up on her knees.

She was so very grateful to the rabbits and Max for helping her to get free

That she offered to let them all share her tea.

With the rabbits all mounted on the big ponies backs

The sun had gone down, it was time to make tracks

Back to the farm and their teas and their beds

And to re-live their adventure in the dreams in their heads.